# About the Author

Lorraine Francis works as a branch librarian in Athlone library. She is married with two sons aged fourteen and eleven. She has also written *Lulu's Tutu*, *Save Our Sweetshop*, *The Origami Bird*, and *Pandora's Lunch Box* for Poolbeg. *The Great Trolley Race* features the children from Barrow Street who first made their appearance in *Save Our Sweetshop*.

Also by Lorraine Francis

Lulu's Tutu
Save Our Sweetshop
The Origami Bird
Pandora's Lunch Box

# Acknowledgements

Thanks, as always, to all at Poolbeg, especially editor Gaye Shortland for her endless encouragement and her faith in happy endings.

For Graham and David, again.

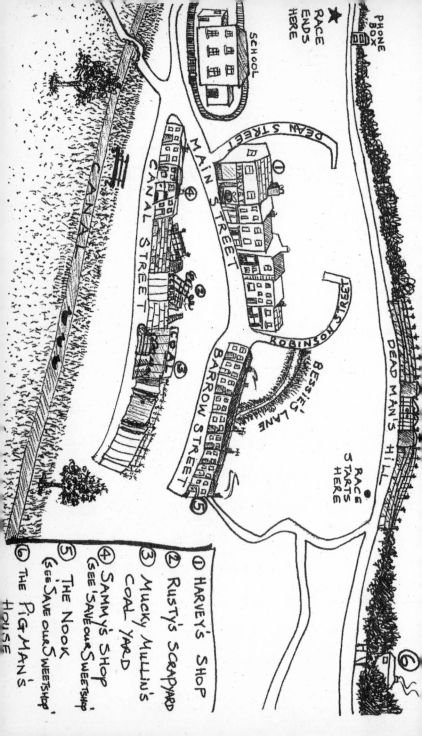

PHONE BOX

RACE ENDS HERE

SCHOOL

DEAN STREET

MAIN STREET

CANAL

CANAL STREET

② COAL

③

BARROW STREET

ROBINSON STREET

BESSIE'S LANE

DEAD MAN'S HILL

RACE STARTS HERE

⑤

⑥

① HARVEY'S SHOP
② RUSTY'S SCRAPYARD
③ MUCKY MULLIN'S COAL YARD
④ SAMMY'S SHOP
    (SEE 'SAVE OUR SWEETSHOP')
⑤ THE NOOK
    (SEE 'SAVE OUR SWEETSHOP')
⑥ THE PIG MAN'S HOUSE

When I was growing up on Barrow Street, long before there were skateboards or micro-scooters, homemade trolleys were all the rage. The first thing you needed to build one was a long, narrow piece of wood; then you got two sets of wheels – pram wheels were best – one set for the front and one for the back. A piece of rope tied to each end of the front axle was used for steering. You could give your trolley a name if you liked; mine was called the *'Hornet'* after my favourite comic, and I wrote it on the wood in black marker. My name is Brendan, by the way, although everyone calls me Benny, for short.

Easter was the time of the Great Trolley Race. As soon as we got our school holidays there were always a few days of furious practice before the Race on Easter Saturday. Of course, trolleys are no use on flat ground so we took them up to a place we called Dead Man's Hill, because of the graveyard there. The best time to practice was in the evening when the road was quiet.

"I don't know why we bother coming all the way up here when Tony's the one who'll be racing," grumbled Frankie as we hauled our trolleys up the hill one evening.

Frankie's trolley was really heavy because it was made out of an old wardrobe door.

"Tony needs people to practice against," said Rita. "It's no good on your own."

Tony Malone was the Barrow Street Trolley Champion. Nobody was faster than Tony who had won the Race for two years in a row.

"Here, you can give me a hand with this," Frankie said to his little brother, Denis, who always tagged along with us.

"Imagine if somebody turned out to be faster than Tony this year," said Denis as he helped Frankie haul the trolley uphill.

"Don't be stupid! Nobody's faster than Tony Malone. Even Comet is like a snail compared to him," said Frankie. (Comet was Frankie's da's greyhound).

Tony was waiting for us at the top of the hill with his trolley tied to a lamppost like a horse in a cowboy film. He was sitting on the edge of the path, fishing for money down a drain with a magnet on the end of a string. Tony was great at finding money; he said it was amazing how much of it got lost down drains. Once, he found something *really* valuable – but that's another story.

There was a small pile of coins on the path beside him, as well as a rusty nail, two bottle tops and a brass button with an eagle on it. He wound up his fishing line and put it back in his pocket. Tony was small and wiry with eyes as black as liquorice and a mop of unruly, dark hair. One of his front teeth was broken from a fall off a trolley and he always had a scab on one of his knees. He picked up the coins and the brass button and tipped the rest of the stuff back down the drain with his foot.

"I think I'll keep this. It might be lucky," he said, polishing the button on his sleeve. "The Roman soldiers had an eagle on their shields." Tony didn't usually give his trolley a name, but this year he had painted the word *'Invincible'* on it in bold black letters.

"That's a great name," said Frankie admiringly. "'Cos it *is* invincible."

"No, it's not!" Denis piped up. "I can see it, plain as anything!"

Frankie gave him a dig with his elbow. *"Invincible*, stupid. Not *invisible,"* he said scornfully. "It means 'unbeatable'."

Rita frowned as she cleaned her glasses with a corner of her cardigan. "Hmm! I think that could be unlucky."

Rita was superstitious about all sorts of things like black cats and walking under ladders. She'd even made her da turn the number 13 on their door around to 31 because she said it was an unlucky number.

"How would it be unlucky?" said Tony as he untied the trolley.

"You know – calling it *'Invincible'*. Pride comes before a fall," Rita warned darkly.

"Rubbish!" scoffed Frankie as we lined our trolleys up across the road. "Nobody believes in that sort of old codswallop!"

"I'm going down to wait at the bottom of the hill. Denis can start the race," Rita said huffily and she marched off, swinging the stopwatch Frankie's da used for timing Comet.

"Ready!" Denis called out. "On your marks . . . get ready . . . I mean . . . on your marks . . . get set . . ." He stooped to pat a small dog that was sniffing around the path.

*"Will you come on!"* Frankie roared at him.

*"Go!"* squeaked Denis.

And we were off! Nice and easy over the bump in the road where the pipe had burst during the frost; a quick swerve around a pothole; then a sharp swing left at the graveyard gates and you were hurtling

downhill like a roller-coaster, with your teeth rattling, your stomach churning, and everything going by in a blur! It was the nearest you could get to flying!

Tony shot into the lead at breakneck speed. Me and Frankie were neck and neck behind. Then the ground began to level off again and Tony stuck out his foot to slow himself down. Sparks flew up off the road from the metal tips on his shoes. He came to a halt beside the phone box at the bottom of the hill with the hair standing up on his head like a Mad Scientist.

"Two seconds off the record!" said Rita triumphantly, as she pressed the button on the stopwatch.

"See! He *is* invincible," Frankie said as we pulled in beside them. "You'll be Champion again this year, Tony. No problem." We hauled the trolleys back up the hill. Denis was sitting on the path playing with the dog. A crowd of kids from the other streets had gathered and we all stood around eyeing each other's trolleys. Georgie Brown, the Robinson Street Champion, had a new set of front wheels on his trolley, the *'Hurricane';* Mossy Moran from Canal Street had built himself a brand new one because his old one got damaged when he crashed during the race the year before. There was no sign of the Dean Street gang, except for Spit Kelly who was trying to read the name on Tony's trolley: *"In-vinc – vinci –"*

*"Invincible,"* said Tony.

"Yeah," said Frankie. "It means 'unbeatable'."

"I wouldn't be so sure about that this

year if I was you," Spit replied with a sly smirk.

Then we heard the sound of loud cheering and the rest of the Dean Street bunch came marching up the hill led by Spit's brother, Johnny, and their three-legged dog, Rinty.

"What are you lot so happy about?" said Mossy Moran. "Anyone'd think ye'd won the race already."

"Show them, Johnny! Show them!" Spit cried, hopping up and down. Johnny raised his hand and the small group parted in the middle like curtains opening on a stage.

There were gasps of admiration all round.

"*Magic!*"

"*Ace!*"

"That's *deadly!*" exclaimed Denis. "It's better than the Batmobile or –"

Frankie clapped his hand over Denis's mouth. "What's that supposed to be?" he demanded.

"What does it look like, stupid?" said Johnny Kelly. "It's a trolley, of course."

But this wasn't just any old trolley. This was a Rolls Royce. It was painted bright red with a covered-in cab for the driver and a black rubber horn like you'd see on

an old-fashioned car. The wheels, with their thick tyres and shiny rims, looked as if they'd just glide over potholes and bumps without a bother, and there was even a brake on the front. In the driver's seat was Sandra Harvey whose father owned the new grocery shop in Main Street.

"She can't run the race for you – she's not from your street," said Mossy Moran.

"Oh, yes, she can!" Spit Kelly retorted. "'Cos the back wall of her house joins onto the side wall of our house. So that makes it all right."

"And my auntie works in their shop," one of the younger kids piped up. "So that makes it double all right."

"But she's a *girl*!" said Frankie. "Girls don't race trolleys!"

Sandra Harvey jumped up from the trolley and came marching over to Frankie. She was tall with brown hair cut short and jaggedy like a boy's. She could beat any of us at arm-wrestling and whenever there was a football match everyone wanted her on their team because she was a great goalie.

"Who says girls don't race trolleys?" she demanded, her hands on her hips.

"Yeah," said Rita indignantly. "Who says?"

Frankie squirmed and his face went as red as Sandra's trolley. "Anyway, trolleys

are supposed to be made out of old bits and pieces," he mumbled. "That one looks like it came out of a shop."

"There's no rules to say what a trolley should look like!" cried Spit Kelly.

"You're just afraid you'll be beaten by a girl, that's all. You're *chicken*," Johnny Kelly jeered.

*"Chicken! Chicken!"* the others taunted, flapping their arms and making clucking noises. Rinty joined in, barking and running around in little wobbly circles that made you think he was going to fall over any minute. Tony sauntered over to the trolley, jingling the coins in his pockets.

"That's not a bad-looking machine," he said, giving the steering rope a tug. "You need a better bit of rope, though."

"That rope's as strong as anything," said

Sandra indignantly. "We use it in our shop for tying up all sorts of things."

Tony shrugged: "Suit yourself. Have you a name for it?"

"Yeah. It's called the *'Humdinger'*," said Sandra.

*"Humdinger?"* Frankie snorted. "What sort of a daft name is that?"

"It means 'a very swift vehicle'," said Sandra, giving Frankie a sharp poke in the ribs. "My uncle's horse is called *Humdinger* and he's always winning races."

"And Sandra's da is giving a prize to whoever wins the race," said Johnny Kelly.

A murmur of excitement went through the crowd.

"What kind of prize?" asked Rita.

"A giant Easter egg. It's in their shop window."

"So you'll all need plenty of practice if you want to win this year," Spit Kelly said as the Dean Street trolleys lined up.

"It'll take more than a swanky red trolley to beat Tony Malone!" Frankie shouted after them as they shot off down the hill.

\* \* \*

*"It's ginormous!"* Georgie Brown exclaimed.

*"Massive!"* said Mossy Moran.

*"Let me see! Let me see!"* Denis squealed as he tried to wriggle through the crowd gathered around Harvey's shop window.

There, among the boxes of cornflakes and the tins of peas, was the biggest Easter egg any of us had ever seen. It was sitting in a straw basket with a big, yellow ribbon

tied in a bow around the middle; a circle of smaller eggs surrounded it like planets orbiting a huge chocolate sun.

"I'd take that sissy ribbon off first thing, if I won it," said Frankie.

"I'd just gobble it all up in one go," Denis said with his nose pressed up against the glass.

"Then you'd be sick, like the time you ate a whole Swiss roll," said Frankie.

"I bet you could fit a thousand of those little ones inside it," Spit Kelly said.

"I don't think Sandra Harvey should get it, even if she wins," said Mossy Moran sulkily. "She could have an egg like that every day if she wanted. I would, if my da owned a shop like that."

Mr Harvey came out of the door of the shop carrying a bundle of mousetraps.

There was a smell off him of hair-oil and cooked ham. He had a stubby pencil stuck behind one ear; a red biro leaked ink through the top pocket of his white shop coat.

"That egg is hand-made from the finest chocolate," he said, grinning at us with his big, square teeth. His bristly, ginger moustache didn't match the hair on his head, which was very black and shiny with hair-oil. "Ah, yes – I remember trolley racing when I was a lad – it was great sport," he said.

"*Sport*?" Frankie hissed. "What does he mean by *sport*? Trolley racing's way more serious than that!"

"Well, may the best man win. Or the best woman, eh?" Mr Harvey said, winking at us before he went back inside.

"Looking at all that chocolate's making me hungry," said Tony. "I'm going down to the Nook to get some marshmallow eggs. Is anyone coming?" The Nook was our local sweetshop; at Easter you could get three marshmallow eggs there for a penny.

"Yeah. I suppose marshmallow eggs'll have to do until we win the big one," Frankie said loudly, so that the others would hear.

"Yah, we'll soon see who'll win!" said Spit Kelly, and he went off whistling through his teeth.

* * *

The Dean Street crowd was up on Dead Man's Hill again the next evening. We tried to pretend we weren't watching as the *Humdinger* shot off down the hill, its sturdy wheels whirring like a well-oiled machine.

"I never saw a trolley go as fast as that," said Denis. "It's *deadly!*"

"Whose side are you on?" snapped Frankie, cuffing him on the ear.

*"Ow!"* squealed Denis. "Leave me

alone! The others are all saying it too. Everyone thinks the *Humdinger's* going to win this year."

"Rubbish! Tony won't let himself be beaten by a girl!"

Rita's eyes narrowed and she shot Frankie a warning look.

Tony gave us his usual cheeky grin, but I saw him giving his lucky brass button a secret rub. And I saw Rita looking at the stopwatch, and I knew by her face that things were not going to be as easy for him this year.

* * *

We met at Tony's house an hour before the start of the Great Trolley Race on Easter Saturday. Rita handed Tony a small, grey, furry thing.

"What are you giving him a dead mouse for?" said Frankie.

"It's a rabbit's foot," said Rita. "I got a loan of it from my granny. She said it brought her luck at bingo last week when she won fifty pounds."

Tony put the rabbit's foot in his pocket and we all trooped out into the hall and opened the front door. Mucky Mullins was trying to turn his coal-truck in the street outside and not making a very good job of it. All of a sudden the truck shot backwards, spilling coal out of the bags on the back. The driver jammed on the brakes just before he hit a lamppost, but not before the truck hit Tony's trolley that was parked at the edge of the path.

"*Aaargh!*" Tony wailed. Denis started to whimper, Rita covered her face with her hands, and Frankie just stood there with his mouth opening and closing like a fish. Mucky Mullins stuck his head out the window of the truck. His face was grimy with coal-dust.

"Any damage?"

"My trolley's banjaxed!" cried Tony, pointing to the buckled back wheel.

"Sorry about that. But it's not the end of the world – you can make one of those old things anytime," Mucky said as he rolled the window back up. He drove off, with the loose bits of coal falling off the back of the truck.

"Huh! So much for your granny's lucky foot! I mean, your granny's lucky rabbit's foot," said Frankie, scowling at Rita. "What'll we do now?"

But Tony was already heading off down the road. "Come on!" he called back over his shoulder. "We'll try Rusty's!"

We raced after him down to the scrap yard along by the canal.

"We need a set of wheels . . . for a trolley . . . quick!" Tony panted as we ran in the gate. The owner, Rusty Roberts, poked around the yard that was jam-packed with girders and gates, bed-ends and bicycles, and other bits of old scrap including a big, black, three-legged pot that looked like a witch's cauldron. He shook his head: "Sorry, folks, I'm afraid you're out of luck today."

"The race starts in twenty minutes," Frankie moaned as we walked back along the canal. "What are we going to do? The others'll think we chickened out!"

Tony skimmed a stone across the canal. "There's no chance of finding any wheels in there either," he said gloomily. People used to dump all sorts of rubbish in the canal before it was cleaned up – but now it was a great place for swimming in the summer.

Rita, who was dawdling along behind and chewing on the end of one of her plaits, said: "I'm going to ask Mrs Brennan if I can take their Billy out for a walk."

"Huh!" Frankie said in disgust. "Trust a girl to think of taking a baby for a walk at a time like this."

A smile began to spread slowly across

Tony's face. "Brilliant!" he said. "Absolutely brilliant!"

"Meet you in Bessie's Lane in five minutes!" Rita called back as she raced away up Canal Street.

* * *

One-year-old Billy Brennan sat on his blanket in Bessie's Lane, drinking a bottle and watching as Tony knelt down and

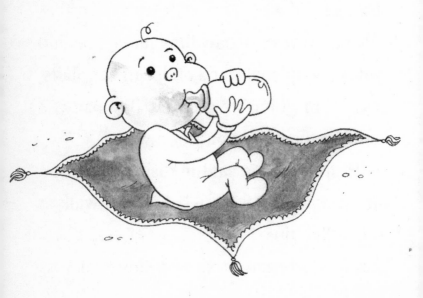

began taking the front wheels off his pram with a screwdriver and spanner.

"We'll hide the pram in the bushes until the race is over," Tony said as he put the wheels on his trolley. "Then we'll come back and put the wheels back on again."

"What about Billy?" said Frankie. "We can't leave *him* in the bushes too."

"We'll have to take him with us," said Rita. "We can carry him in his blanket. And we'd better hurry – there's only five minutes left before the race starts."

Billy rolled around in the blanket gurgling with glee as we carried him up Dead Man's Hill.

"It's a good job he can't talk or he'd tell on us," said Denis.

"It's a pity he can't walk, though," grumbled Frankie. "He weighs a ton."

There was a big crowd up on the hill; some of them were holding up banners with the names of their streets on them.

We put Billy down on the path and Rita gave him a rattle to play with.

"He can be our lucky mascot," she said.

"Huh! If you ask me, all this talk about

things being lucky has brought us nothing but bad luck!" said Frankie.

Mr Harvey was at the starting line holding a red flag.

"What's he doing here? It's no fun when there's grown-ups around," Frankie scowled.

"I know," Rita agreed. "But I suppose he *is* giving the winner a prize."

The Dean Street crowd started chanting: "*Ready, steady, go, go, go! Sandra's fast, and the rest are slow!*" and honking the *Humdinger's* horn.

"*To-ny is the best, ten times faster than the rest!*" we shouted from the other side of the road.

Mr Harvey raised the flag. A hush fell on the crowd, except for Billy who was bashing his rattle off the path. Rita put him lying down on the blanket with his bottle.

"You can keep an eye on him till the race is over," she said to Denis.

"On your marks . . ." Mr Harvey boomed. The trolley racers stared straight ahead, their knuckles white as they gripped the steering ropes. It was so quiet you could have heard a pin drop. Bubblegum popping somewhere in the crowd sounded like an explosion.

"Get set . . ." Mr Harvey said, going up on his toes like someone trying to look over a wall. The flag dropped. *"Go!"*

The Great Trolley Race was on! The *Humdinger* took off like a rocket, its powerful wheels bouncing over the bumps and potholes like a speedboat through water.

Tony was next with the others close behind. The crowd surged downhill after them. Spit Kelly galloped along, slapping his hand against his side like a cowboy trying to make his horse go faster. Rinty hobbled after him, panting as he tried to keep up.

"That bloomin' *Humdinger's* going to win! I know it! I just know it!" moaned Frankie.

*"Come on, Tony!"* we cried at the tops of our voices as Tony began to lag further behind.

Sandra pulled hard on the steering rope as she took the sharp turn after the graveyard gates. All of a sudden the rope snapped on one side. The trolley wavered all over the road as she tried to steer it back on course. She managed to straighten it up a bit, but then it veered sideways and one

wheel mounted the path. Sandra hung on grimly, but the trolley tipped over and tossed her out onto the path.

*"Get up! Get up! He's passing you out!"* Spit Kelly shrieked as Tony whizzed by.

"Oh, my arm!" moaned Sandra as she rolled on the ground.

Rita and I ran over and helped her up as a great cheer came from the bottom of the hill.

"It's not fair! Sandra would've won if that blooming thing hadn't turned over!" said Spit Kelly, giving the *Humdinger* a kick. He looked as if he were going to cry.

Frankie came bounding over. "Tony's done it again! It's a hat-trick!" he crowed as Mr Harvey led Sandra away, moaning and holding onto her arm.

"Well, that's it, I suppose," said Rita.

Things felt a bit flat, like a drink with all the fizz gone out of it.

"That was hard luck on Sandra," said Tony as he came back up the hill with Denis sitting proudly on the trolley. "I knew that rope was a bit dodgy."

"Nah," said Frankie, clapping him on the back. "I knew all along you were invincible."

"I suppose we'd better put the wheels back on Billy's pram," said Tony. "Or Mrs Bren –"

"Billy!" cried Rita, cutting him off. "Where's Billy?"

"I thought you were supposed to be minding him!" Frankie yelled at Denis.

"I forgot all about him!" Denis snivelled. "I wanted to see the race too, so I did!"

We ran back up the hill. The blanket and the empty bottle were on the path, but there was no sign of Billy.

"He's gone! Oh, what are we going to do?" Rita wailed, twisting her plaits round and round her fingers. "Mrs Brennan'll go mad!"

"He can't be too far away," said Frankie. "He can't walk, remember?"

"Babies are great at crawling," said Denis. "Our teacher told us a story about a baby that crawled for *miles* and had an adventure."

"Will you shut up!" Frankie snapped. "It's all your fault he's gone!"

Then Tony called out from the other side of the hill: "Over here! I found his rattle! And one of his socks!"

We ran over to join him. "There's the other sock," Denis whimpered, his eyes wide as saucers. "Inside the . . . P . . . Pig Man's gate. He must've squeezed through the bars."

We opened the gate cautiously. We were all a bit wary of the big, red-faced Pig Man who went around from house to house on a donkey and cart collecting leftover food for his pigs. We could hear the sound of high-pitched squealing as we crept up the muddy lane.

"A boy in my class said the Pig Man has a cage where he keeps children to fatten them up for Christmas," Denis whispered. "He could've put Billy in it."

"Then we'll do a swap with him for *you*!" Frankie said, and Denis started whingeing again. He was a great crier.

"Oh no!" Rita groaned as we turned a corner. We all stopped and stared. Wallowing in a big patch of oozing mud under an apple-tree were six little piglets. Denis peered closely. "One of those baby pigs looks awful like –"

"Billy!" wailed Rita.

Billy rolled over and over in the mud, squealing just like one of the piglets.

"He's mucky all over!" exclaimed Denis. "Every single bit of him!"

"Ugh! I'm not picking him up. No way!" said Frankie.

"The Pig Man!" Denis whimpered. "The Pig Man is coming!"

The Pig Man came squelching down the lane in huge, mucky wellingtons with a bucket swinging from each of his big, loose hands. A very clean-looking pig trotted along beside him.

"Will you look at that, Grunty?" the Pig Man said with a laugh that sounded like water going down a drain. The pig made a noise that sounded a bit like a laugh too.

"That pig understands English!" said Denis.

The Pig Man emptied the buckets onto the ground. The piglets ran over and began eating noisily. Billy crawled after them.

"Don't tell me he's going to eat it too!" groaned Frankie.

The Pig Man bent down and scooped Billy up under his arm. Denis yelped like a frightened puppy.

"We'd better give the babby a dip before his mammy sees him," the Pig Man said, jerking his head for us to follow him.

In the farmhouse kitchen that smelt like a cake shop, Betty, the Pig Man's wife, washed Billy in a tin bath beside the fire.

"*Eeeek!*" Billy squealed, like one of the piglets. Betty gave us red lemonade and biscuits and some fresh eggs for Mrs Brennan.

"So she won't be too cross with ye," she said. Then she put Billy's dirty clothes in a bag and wrapped him up in one of her big cardigans to keep him warm. And Billy cried '*Eeeekk! Eeeekk! Eeeekk!*' all the way home.

\* \* \*

Sandra Harvey broke her arm in the Big Race. But it wasn't her wrestling arm so she didn't mind too much.

"You lot haven't heard the last of the *Humdinger* either," she said as we signed her plaster cast. "It'll be back in action next year, so you'd better watch out." We didn't get into too much trouble with Mrs Brennan either – she said that if Tony was so handy with a screwdriver he could come and fix a few things around the house for her. Though she soon got fed up with Billy squealing like a piglet all the time.

And we got a nice surprise on Easter Sunday morning when we opened the giant Easter egg: inside it were loads of little eggs wrapped in shiny, gold paper. Rita shared them out and we sat munching them in the shed in Frankie's yard, which we used as a den whenever Comet wasn't in there. He was running in a big greyhound race that day.

"I'm going to ask Mammy if I can have a pig for a pet," said Denis, putting two of the little eggs in his mouth at the same time.

"Don't be daft! A pig isn't the right sort of animal for a pet," Frankie replied.

"Yes, it is!" Denis said, dribbling chocolate down his chin. "Grunty's a pet pig – he sleeps in a basket in the kitchen at night. And he can give you the paw."

"Pigs have *trotters*, not *paws*," Frankie said, pulling Denis's hair.

"*Ow*! I'm telling Mammy on you!" Denis said, and he began to cry.

"You're such a *baby!*" Frankie said scornfully.

"There's nothing wrong with being a baby," Rita said. "If it wasn't for a certain baby called Billy Brennan, we wouldn't be here tucking into all this yummy chocolate. I think we should give three cheers for babies and their trusty prams – *Hip! Hip!* –"

"*Hooray!*" we all cried, and Denis cheered loudest of all.

## THE END